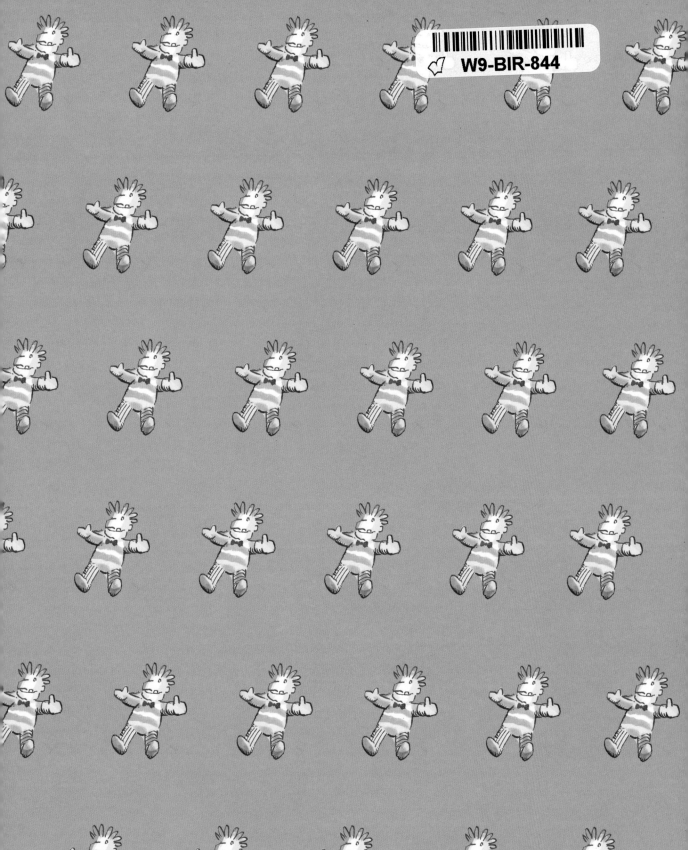

For Jill Grinberg
—J.M.

With many thanks to Johnny Marciano and the team at Akashic!
—P.H.

Published by Akashic Books
Words © 2021 by Johnny Marciano
Illustrations © 2021 by Paul Hoppe

ISBN: 978-1-61775-927-7
Library of Congress Control Number: 2021935243

First printing
Printed in China

Black Sheep/Akashic Books
Brooklyn, New York
Twitter: @AkashicBooks
Facebook: AkashicBooks
E-mail: info@akashicbooks.com
Website: www.akashicbooks.com

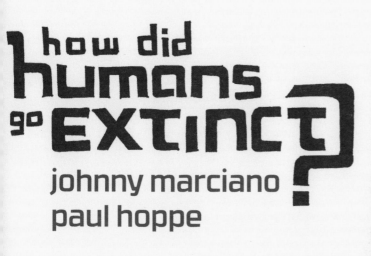

how did humans go EXTINCT?

johnny marciano
paul hoppe

HUMAN AND BABY
C. 10 MILLION YEARS AGO

Plib was so excited. Today he was going on a class trip. To the Natural History Museum!

Some kids loved the exhibits on outer space.

Others liked the room of evolution.

Could Nøørfbløøks really have descended from frogs?

But Plib's favorite displays were of . . .

HUMANS!
Did they have fur? Feathers? Scales?
No one knows for sure!

Plib loved humans. His favorite book was *How Do Humans Say Good Night?* His favorite movie was *Human Park*. And his favorite stuffie was a human named Frank.

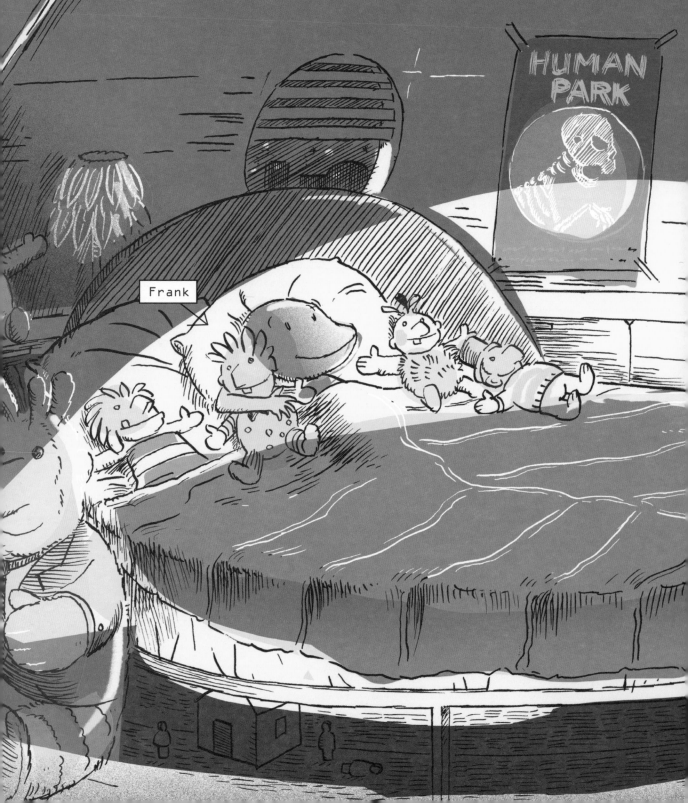

Frank

At the museum, Plib's classmates learned
many fun—and bizarre!—human facts.

Humans came out of their mothers
ALREADY ALIVE!

Disgusting!

Humans had beaks made of FLESH

Eww, gross!

I'd never want to
meet a human!

Humans ate other ANIMALS!

Plib didn't care
if the other kids
thought humans
were monsters.
He wanted to
meet one.

On the long ride home, Plib couldn't help but wonder:
What happened to all those poor humans?

At dinner, he couldn't eat his food.

And at bedtime, he couldn't concentrate on the story
his mother was reading. She asked what was wrong,
and Plib told her about his school trip.

Then he asked the question he couldn't stop thinking about:

Mom, how did humans go extinct?

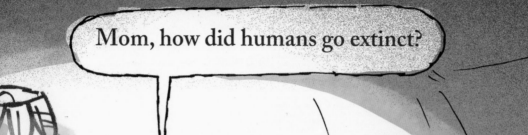

Mom thought the answer was too disturbing to hear, but Plib wouldn't stop asking.

Mom sighed.
Then she told him.

"Some say the humans created so much pollution that they heated up the planet. Half the Earth flooded under the melted ice, the other half burned, and what was left got destroyed in the storms that followed."

Plib clutched Frank tightly.

"But when that started to happen, wouldn't the humans have just stopped what they were doing?"

Mom agreed, and told him a different theory.

Others think that humans made each other go extinct. They could never admit when they were wrong and blamed each other for all of their problems. Some archaeologists think humans *liked* to hate each other.
NUMBER
1

Plib eyed Frank suspiciously. *Very* suspiciously.

"The craziest idea of all is that they just stopped taking care of each other. Some humans took whatever they could get, and left nothing for the rest."

Plib was devastated. Could humans have really been that bad?
He wagged a finger at Frank.

"I think the TRUTH is that the humans figured it all out. They might have been beasts, they might have had noses, they might have done bad things, but in the end, I believe they all came together and learned how to survive together in peace and harmony for many millions of years."

Plib smiled, thinking about the happy humans.
Mom turned out the light and kissed him.
But before she could leave, Plib stopped her.

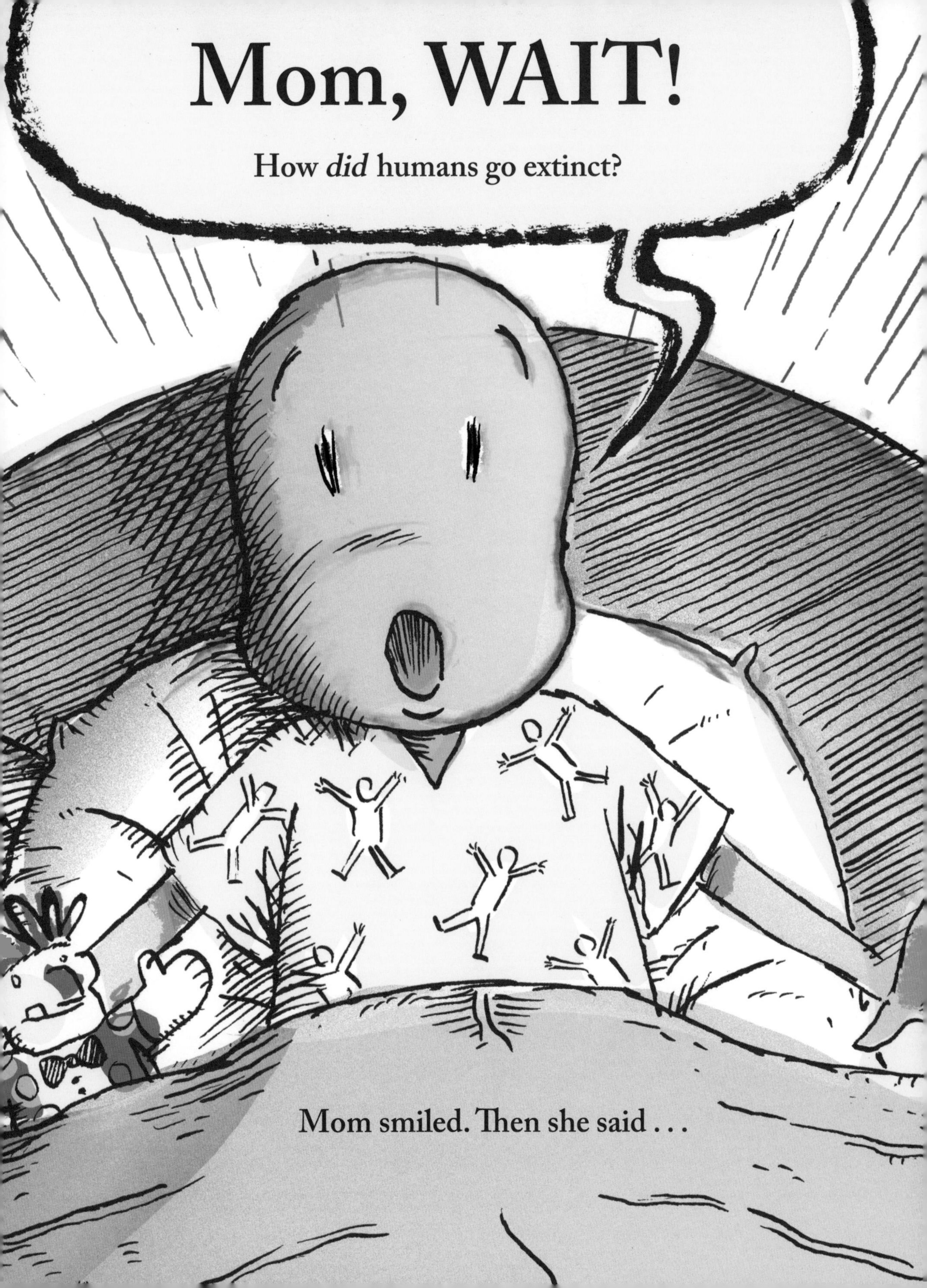

Mom smiled. Then she said . . .

"Well, what I like to think is that a GIANT ASTEROID crashed into Earth."

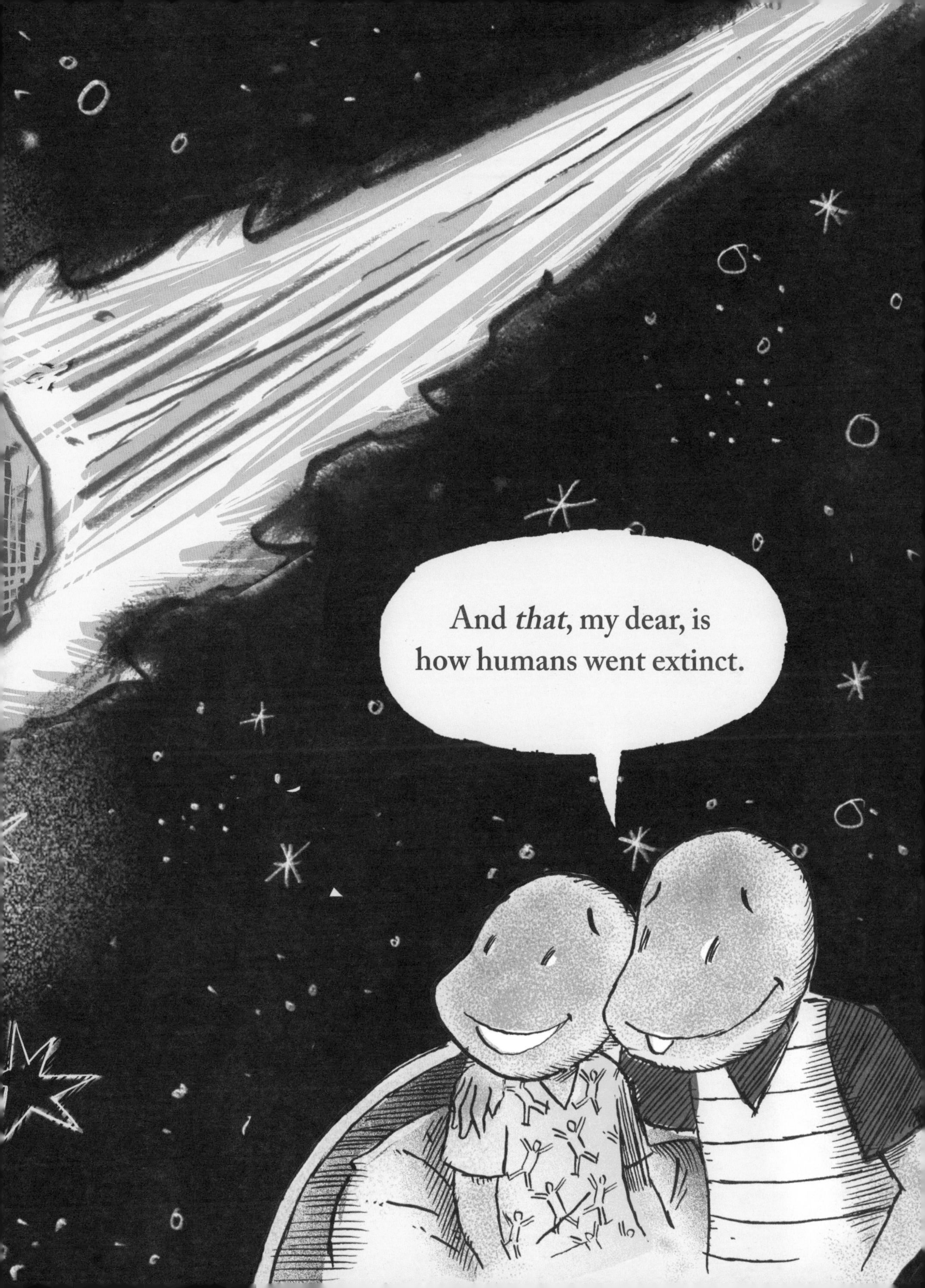
And *that*, my dear, is how humans went extinct.

Plib kissed Frank, and then they went to sleep.

THE END